Bedtime, Little Ones!

Claire Freedman ★ Gail Yerrill

It's been such a happy day playing,
The setting sun glows golden red.
The little ones run home for supper,
For soon it will be time for bed.

Mummy Mouse smiles
at her children,
"Time for bed, when you've
finished your teas!"
"We're not at all tired!"
the mice chorus,
But someone's asleep
in her cheese!

It's bathtime – five rabbits are splashing,
Having fun in their big bubbly tub!
"We love to splish-splosh!" they tell Mummy,
As she gives each small bunny a scrub.

Mummy Rabbit is
drying her bunnies,
And counting them,
"One, two, three, four..."

Then she giggles,
"Wait – somebody's missing!
There should be just
one bunny more!"

The little ones snuggle round Grandpa,
As he reads to them tales from his book.
"And another!" cries one little badger.
"There's a great story here, Grandpa – look!"

Mummy Squirrel says,
"Bedtime, my babies,
Hear the sleepy-train
calling choo-choo!"
But one little squirrel's
not sleepy,
She still wants to
play peek-a-boo!

The little bears gaze at the night sky,
As silver bright stars start to peep.
"One, two, three, ZZZZ!" someone's snoring.
Star counting has sent him to sleep!

Little Rabbit is searching all over.
"Oh no!" he cries. "Where's Little Ted?
I must find my cuddly bear, Mummy,
I can't sleep without him in bed!"

All the animals have their own teddies,
To cuddle and snuggle up tight.
With each of their soft toys beside them,
They're sure to sleep soundly all night!

As Mummy Mouse
tucks up each baby,
She whispers, "Goodnight,
sleepy-head!"
Then Little Mouse
copies her Mummy,
And she tucks up her
own toy in bed.

The hedgehogs are drifting to sleep now,
As Daddy sings sweet lullabies,
But one little hedgehog is singing along,
"Tra-la-la! I love Daddy!" he cries.